BEN'S BRAND-NEW GLASSES

First published in 1987
by Faber and Faber Limited
3 Queen Square, London WC1N 3AU

Photoset by Parker Typesetting Service Leicester
Printed in Great Britain by
W. S. Cowell Ltd Ipswich

Text and illustrations © Carolyn Dinan 1987

British Library Cataloguing in Publication Data

Dinan, Carolyn
Ben's brand-new glasses.
I. Title
823'.914 [J]   PZ7
ISBN 0–571–14567–1

For Gangadhar

BEN'S BRAND-NEW GLASSES

Carolyn Dinan

faber and faber

LONDON · BOSTON

Ben came home from his new school in a very bad temper.

'I hate that school,' he said. 'I don't know anybody and I can't find anything and I'm always getting lost. I wish we'd never moved house. I don't like living here at all.'

'You'll soon make friends,' said his mother.

'I won't,' said Ben. 'And I've got a headache and a tummyache and a pain all down my legs. I'll never get to school tomorrow.'

'But you aren't going to school tomorrow,' said Mrs Bell.
'At least not in the morning. I was going to take you to
have your eyes tested but perhaps you'd better stay in bed
instead. I don't suppose you'll want any supper . . .'

'Well, I'll have my supper and that might make me feel better,'
said Ben quickly. 'I think I'm a bit better already.
I'm bound to be all right by tomorrow.'

It was fun at the optician's.
Ben had to look very hard at lots of coloured lights and shapes, and tell Miss Bright what he saw.

'Well done, Ben,' she said.
'Now can you read the letters on this screen?'
'That's easy,' said Ben.
'I know all my letters. I can't
see the little ones, though.
They're all fuzzy.'

Miss Bright put a funny black spectacle frame on Ben's
nose and slipped round glass lenses into it.

'Oh!' said Ben. 'I can see the little letters now!'

'Good,' said Miss Bright. 'I'm going to make you some
glasses so that you will be able to see just as clearly
all the time. Would you like that?'

'No,' said Ben. The little letters weren't very interesting.
It didn't seem worth all the fuss.

'Choose a frame, Ben,' said Miss Bright. 'And I'll have
your brand-new glasses ready for you next week.'

One week later the glasses were ready.
'Here you are, Ben,' said Miss Bright. 'Let's see how they feel.'
Ben put them on.
'They feel horrible,' he said.
'They're lovely,' said his mother. 'They really suit you.
You look very smart in them.'
'I don't feel it,' said Ben. 'They're heavy on my nose
and they hurt my ears.'
'You'll soon get used to them,' smiled Miss Bright, 'and then
you'll forget you're wearing them.'
'I won't,' said Ben.

When Ben got home he ran upstairs to the bathroom, climbed on the laundry basket and looked in the mirror.

'I look awful,' he thought. 'I don't look like me at all.'

He put the glasses in his pocket and went slowly downstairs.

Ben had his lunch and then it was time to go to school.

'Put your smart new glasses on,' said his mother. 'You'll need them this afternoon.'

Ben stared at her in horror. 'I'm not going to school in THOSE,' he said.

'Why not? They look so nice on you. Hurry up now, we don't want to be late.'

'I don't need to wear them walking along.'

'Well, take them with you and wear them for lessons. Look! They've even got a special red leather case to keep them in, so they don't get broken.'

Ben hid his glasses in his shoe-bag. 'I can't wear them now,' he thought. 'Everyone will laugh at me . . . and Miss Murphy might not recognize me. She hasn't known me very long.'

All the way home from school Ben worried.
  'What if Mum asks if I've worn my glasses? What about
tomorrow . . . and the next day? I wish I'd never got the
beastly things,' he thought bitterly. 'If only I could
lose them . . .'

'Lose them!'

Ben stood still. His mother walked on ahead and round the corner. He pulled the glasses case out of his pocket, threw it over a hedge and ran after his mother as fast as he could.

Mrs Bell had made a cake for tea. She gave Ben a big slice.
'Where are your glasses?' she asked.

'I think I've lost them,' said Ben sadly.

'Oh Ben!' said his mother crossly. 'You can't have lost them
so soon.'

Just then the doorbell rang. A girl stood on the doorstep.
She was holding a very muddy red glasses case.

'I'm Sue from the farm,' she said. 'I think this belongs to
you. Don't look so worried, your glasses aren't broken. We
did get a surprise, though, when they flew over the hedge into our
field. Poor old Saffron nearly bolted.'

Sue stayed for tea, and after tea they went to see Saffron and gave him an apple.

'You can have a ride if you like,' said Sue.

'I'd love it,' said Ben excitedly. 'Thank you!'

'Better wear your glasses,' said Sue. 'You want to see where you're going.'

'All right,' Ben agreed. 'I'll wear them for that.'

The next day was fine and sunny, and Miss Murphy took the children to the river for Nature Study. 'Let's see how many different insects and plants we can find,' she said.

Ben peered into the water and something darted past among the strands of weed. He leaned forward to see better and as he did so, his glasses slipped out of his pocket and fell in the river with a gentle splash. Ben watched, open-mouthed, as the red case disappeared beneath the surface.

'It wasn't my fault,' he thought virtuously as they set off back to school with Miss Murphy. 'I couldn't risk drowning just to rescue a pair of glasses.'

Ben's mother didn't agree. She was very annoyed when he arrived home without his glasses.

'Why didn't you ask Miss Murphy for help? Really, Ben! You should have had more sense.'

Just then the doorbell rang.

A boy stood on the doorstep holding a fishing net in one hand. In the other hand he held something greenish and slimy.

'I'm Ram from the corner shop,' he said. 'Are these your glasses?'

'No,' said Ben firmly.

'Yes,' said Ben's mother. 'And thank you! How did you find them?'

'I fished them out of the river,' said Ram proudly. 'I'm afraid they need a good wash.'

Ram stayed for tea and after tea he took Ben fishing.
'We'll put our catch back afterwards,' he said. 'It's
no fun living in a jam-jar. Better wear your glasses.
You want to be able to see the fish.'

'All right,' said Ben. 'I'll wear them for that.'

Ben woke up in a very good mood.

'Saturday today,' he sang. 'No school today.'

'I'm going to a Jumble Sale,' said his mother. 'Like to come?'

'No, thank you,' said Ben. 'I don't like Jumble Sales.'

'You have to be careful at Jumble Sales,' said Mr Bell. 'The only one I went to, I put my jacket down for a moment and someone sold it for 5p.'

Ben put his glasses in his pocket.

'Perhaps I'll come after all,' he said.

The Jumble Sale was crowded with people, all pushing and shoving and waving clothes in the air. Ben wriggled through to the Fancy Goods stall and put the glasses down on the table.

'I'll just leave them there for a moment,' he thought. 'If somebody buys them, it can't be helped.'

'Ben!' called his mother. 'Come over here. I want to see if this jersey fits you.'

Ben ran over and tried it on. He found a judo suit too and a space-helmet. He forgot all about the glasses.

'I do like Jumble Sales!' Ben sighed happily when they got home. 'They make you hungry, though. Is lunch nearly ready?'

'Yes,' said Mrs Bell. 'Pop your glasses on and lay the table . . . What's the matter, Ben?'

Just then the doorbell rang.

A large lady stood on the doorstep.

'I'm Mary Lee from the Fancy Goods stall,' she said. 'I was packing up and I found these . . .'

Ben gazed at Mrs Lee in bewilderment.

'How did you know they were mine?' he asked. 'Why does everyone always know they belong to me?'

Mrs Lee laughed. 'Your name and address are inside the case. If you put your glasses on, you'll see.'

Mrs Lee stayed for lunch. 'I'm very glad we've got to know each other,' she said. 'My grand-daughter is coming round this afternoon. Would Ben like to come to the cinema with us?'

'Yes, please!' said Ben. 'I'd love to.'

'Better wear your glasses,' said Mrs Lee, 'or you won't be able to see the film.'

'I'll wear them for that!' said Ben.

Mrs Bell worked late on Monday, so Ben and his father went
to the supermarket.

'Wear your glasses, Ben,' said Mr Bell. 'Then you can tell
me where everything is.'

Ben put his glasses on and zipped his anorak up to his nose.
He hoped he wouldn't bump into anyone from his school.

'There's that little boy from your class,' said his father.
'Tim, isn't it? Look, he's waving to you. Now, where's
my shopping list . . .?'

Ben took his glasses off quickly and put them in the bottom of the trolley. It was hard to see them against the wire mesh. Ben's father didn't see them at all. He put a large packet of washing powder on top of them and Ben waited for the scrunch, but nothing happened.

'They must have extra-tough glass,' thought Ben gloomily. 'I'd better just leave them where they are. If I move everything to take them out Dad will make me wear them.'

'That's a good job done,' said Mr Bell as they unpacked the shopping. 'Where are your glasses, Ben?'

Ben took the case out of his pocket and opened it. It was empty.

'Oh,' said Ben, remembering.

Just then the doorbell rang.

Tim and his family stood on the doorstep.

'We found your glasses,' said Tim. 'I saw you wearing them at the supermarket, but you left them in your trolley. Why don't you wear them at school?'

Ben's father gave him a long, hard look but didn't say anything.

Tim's family stayed for tea, and all through tea Tim stared at Ben's glasses.

'Look at those frames,' he said. 'Are they real silver?'

'I expect so,' said Ben.

'Can I try them on?' asked Tim. 'Oooh! Everything looks funny.'

'That's because I'm the only person in the world who can see through them,' said Ben.

'Pheeewww!' Tim whistled. 'Let's walk home together after school tomorrow and look for conkers. You wear your glasses and I bet we find hundreds.'

'All right,' said Ben. 'I'll wear them for that.'

Ben ran all the way to school next morning and got there early. But Miss Murphy was late.

'I'm very sorry, children, but I just had to call in at the optician for these,' she said when she arrived at last.
'I couldn't wait another day for them. What do you think of my grand new glasses, everyone? I can see you all as clear as could be now, and you can take that bubble gum out of your mouth AT ONCE, Angela. I can even see right to the back of the class!'

All the children were very impressed.

'I've got glasses too,' said Ben suddenly.

'No, you haven't,' said Maria. 'You don't wear glasses.'

'Yes, he does,' said Tim. 'AND he's got special ones with real silver frames. Go on, Ben, show them!'

Ben opened his bag. He took his glasses out of their case and carefully put them on.

'Well!' said Miss Murphy. 'Aren't we a fine couple, Ben? Sit down, children. You can see Ben's beautiful new glasses from your own chairs. And today we'll have a lesson all about our eyes.'

So Ben wore his glasses all day and suddenly he discovered something very surprising.

He could see.

He could see everything that Miss Murphy wrote on the board and he didn't have to ask anyone for help. He could catch the ball easily at games time and he found his way round the school with no trouble at all and soon knew everybody.

'I think my glasses must be a bit magic,' he told his mother one night. 'I have a great time at school now that I wear them.'

'I know!' Mrs Bell gave him a hug. 'And what a lot of friends we've made too. I really like your new glasses, Ben, don't you?'

'Yes,' said Ben. And he put them safely away in their case by his bed and went to sleep.